BlackRose Presents: Deception

I0550365

Deception:

By:

Talisha Mallory

BlackRose Presents: Deception

Acknowledgements:

First and foremost I would like to thank my Lord and Savior for blessing me with this gift. Without HIM none of this would be possible.

I would also like to give up mad kudos to Mrs. Fiordaliza Charles. Much love and appreciation

My mother Sheila Harden I love you and miss u...

My grandmother Ms. Juanita Harden I love you and miss u...

Dedication:

I dedicate this to my mother Ms. Sheila Harden. I miss you momma

Introduction:

This book started out as a challenge. This book sat in the vault for years on end until one I put it on Facebook. The day I put it on Facebook was the day I realized that my gift has been lying dormant. Before I forget what I came here to do: I bring you Gladys whom is Mar'Shaye's mother and the head of the household. Then you have Mar'Shaye a very naïve 18 yr. old that believes in love. You will meet Tanesha, Mar'Shaye's sister. Who just happens to show up outta the blue one day? You will then meet Tariq, umph with his sexy self. I don't wanna give too much away but with Ms. Gladys leading the family, all hell finna break lose....

Dew Drops

I need to ask u a question and that question is....

Can u take this journey with me thru the dew drops....?

At the end of the trail there is something waiting only for u....

Don't be afraid I wouldn't do anything to hurt you or make you feel unsafe....

I promise just take my hand and take this journey with me thru the dew drops....

I need to ask you a question and that question is.....

Do you find me attractive....?

Do you find me worthy of your essence....?

Am I worthy of your time and patience....?

Can I be where ever you are emotionally....?

If so let me take your mind on this journey thru the dew drops.......

BlackRose Presents: Deception

I need to ask you a question and that question is.....

This one being the most troubling; if u had a choice before the choice was made......

Would you journey with me thru the dew drops....?

Would you hold my hand and tell me that everything would be just fine wrapped in your arms.....

Would you whisper in my ear and reassure me that this journey is just beginning.....

If so please......

Take my hand and let's journey thru the dew drops......

One final question and that question is.....

Once we get to the end of this trail....

Whatever happens.....?

Can you do me one favor.......?

Can you make love to me at the end of this journey and lay me amongst the dew drops....

BlackRose Presents:

Deception

By:

Talisha Mallory

Chapter1

Why it is the simplest things in life are the hardest...? Why are the most difficult things so hard to get sometimes...? Why it is no one seems to know the truth when it's time to bare your soul....? Well, maybe some of these questions you can help answer throughout my life changing circumstance:

Hi, my name is Mar 'Shaye' and my story unfolds like so: I was at a party the other night with my girls: Shanei', Tanesha, Cameron, & Monet'. We were all just kicking it like we always do when this fine ass chocolate man walked up and was like "What's up ladies, enjoying your night...?" Now I was too busy studying this brothers fine physique and his gorgeous lips. I had no idea that my girls had spoken up until I felt Monet' nudge me in my side. I relaxed and said "Yea, I'm enjoying my nite now that you've arrived..." he smiled and he had the most perfect teeth and the cutest dimples. I damn near forgot I was supposed to be waiting till marriage to enjoy pleasure.

He leaned over and said "My name is Tariq and your names are....?" and my girls rushed right in and started speaking all at once. I waited and took in the rest of him. He stood at least 6'5" he was all muscle or what I thought was muscle. He had the most intoxicating grey eyes for a man of African-American descent. He had a full pair of lips that I just wanted to suck on like green apple jolly ranchers. I kept venturing down further and further and I was having thoughts about this man that I shouldn't. When I felt another nudge, "Oh, I'm sorry; I'm Mar 'Shaye'" he smiled and said "What a beautiful name for such a beautiful woman" Now don't get me wrong I am all woman but I'm only 18 so that made me feel special as I said "Thank You" with my mocha skin all hot and flushed I could of sworn he seen me turn red. He then said "Well, excuse me ladies and do enjoy your evening" We all said in unison "We Will" like the love starved teenagers we were well at least some of us.

As soon as he walked away Shanei' spoke up first which was likely being she was the oldest. "Girl he was show paying you a lot of attention...." she said in a huff like I cared. Then she turned to my sister and said "Tanesha what you think...? How old do you think he is...?" and she went on asking questions for what seemed like hours. When she finally took a breather my sister said "Look Shanei' FYI my sister *happens to be a very smart individual and if she has kept her sanity this long around men then I'm damn proud of her and if she chooses to lose her sanity and hump that man's brains out then that's cool with me to. Just leave her alone and mind your own damn business...damn" and Shanei' did just that and shut the fuck up and left me the fuck alone. Now let me help you out with something when my sister speaks of ones sanity as she puts it; she's talking about my virginity. Lord knows it's been hell to keep with all the clothes burning I've been doing with all my previous boyfriends. I just wasn't ready and I hated for someone to pressure me into something I just wasn't ready to be pushed into.*

Well later on that nite while I'm climbing into the car with my sister I felt someone touch my hand and when I looked up it was none other than Tariq he simply said "I just wanted you to have my number just in case" he smiled and strolled away. When we got home momma was sitting up waiting on us as usual. It didn't matter how late we came home she always sat up to make sure we arrived home safely. I kissed momma good night and I went upstairs to get undressed for bed. When I emptied my pockets Tariq's number was the first thing I saw I was tempted to call right away but I put it off for later date. I then crawled into bed and went to sleep.

That morning I woke up to the smell of bacon, homemade biscuits and whatever else momma was cooking. I stretched and got out of bed and proceeded to wash my face and brush my teeth. I headed down stairs when my sister wiz past me in a blur of colors. We joined momma in the kitchen

I so loved my momma for so many different reasons; one being she was my everything especially after daddy left. I think I was about 8yrs. old and my sister wasn't really around then I'll explain that later.

Momma turned around and smiled her perfect smile and said to me "Well baby, now that you have officially graduated from high school, what's in your future...?" I thought about it and said "Honestly momma I don't know...." momma smiled and said "Take your time baby, you'll figure it out" then my sister jumped right in and said "Well what are we doing for your Birthday...?" she smiled her mischievous smile therefore I knew she was up to something. I smiled back and said "What do you have in mind, my most adorable and precious sister" she smiled and looked at momma and momma returned the smile and said "What, what has got momma smiling so big...? What did you do...?" I asked curious beyond reason and then they both blurted in unison "Nothing" with a much needed chuckle. I just looked at them both and smiled-something was up.

Part 2

Now let me tell you something about my sister I think you should know and help you understand her a little better. My sister came into my life after daddy left she had to be around 10yrs. old at the time. Yea, you heard right she just showed up on momma's stoop with a letter and an Aldi's bag full of her belongings.

Momma didn't push her away it didn't bother momma any to see this girl dirty with no shoes on her feet and the fact that she smelled of piss. All mommas' words not my own. Momma took her by the hand and led her inside and sat her down on the sofa and said "What's your name child...?" and she responded "Tanesha, Ma'am" momma said she asked her where she lived and she said the poor child said "Oklahoma, Ma'am" mind you we live in

17

*the Chicago area way out in the suburbs.
So momma said she asked her how did she
get way to Chicago and Tanesha replied
"My momma brought me ma'am" so
momma being momma asked her, her
mother's name and Tanesha replied "Ms.
Shannon Whelks, Ma'am" momma shook
her head in disgust and said "Child do
your mother happen to have a number....?"
Tanesha shook her head no Tanesha went
on telling momma everything she thought
she needed to know.*

*Momma said she gave Tanesha
something to eat and proceeded to run her
some bath water. She then gave her a set
of my pajamas and sent her to bed. Once
Tanesha had something in her belly, bathe,
and off to bed that's when momma decided
to open the letter. Momma didn't give me
everything but she did tell me I had a new*

sister and left it at that I never asked any questions although I'm still curious.

"Hello, where are you....? Are you thinking about tall, dark, and sexy...?" I snapped out of the past and looked at my sister with the most evil look I could muster but my smile fucked it up. "No, I was thinking about my birthday in a couple of weeks and what you and momma got planned" I seemed to smile in spite of it all "So," momma said placing my breakfast in front of us "Who is the lucky guy...?" she continued. I smiled and said "How you know he lucky momma?" she looked at me knowing damn well my every thought and move and said "I feel it and you smiling to boot. So he must be special" I kind of a nodded and said my blessing and shoved a piece of bacon in my mouth

like I was on one of those Twix commercials.

I returned to my room to get in the shower so I could get dressed Tanesha was taking me somewhere special today. As I was getting out the shower my phone rang and it was none other than Monet' talking loud and out of control "I saw that shit last night..." I kind of looked at the phone and said "What shit you talking about...?" she then sucked her teeth and said "I saw that nigga slip you his number I ain't blind, so what I was a few cars back" Damn, she nosy as hell shit, I can't even get a number now-a-days "Is that why you called me...?" I asked. She smacked her lips and said "No, I called yo' stank ass to see if you called him yet...?" Oh, hell naw she was getting on my last nerve "Nail I ain't called him yet and why in hell you wanna know

Monet'...?" she had the nerve to catch an attitude "Look if you not gone call him then give me the number, you don't know what to do with a man anyways..." she replied. This was getting so old and really fast-so what I'm still a virgin. These bitches act like it's a crime to be safe and wait shit out. So I simply said "Hell nail I'm not giving you his number and so what I'm still a virgin. I can always learn how to please my man if and when it comes down to it" she sucked her teeth yet again "Whatever," I was so pissed at this point I hung up on her ass-fuckin haters.

Chapter 3

I threw on my Dereon jeans and I snatched up one of my mid-riff tops that had my name across the breast and my white on white air force ones. I grabbed my cell, my keys, and my purse and was down the stairs I kissed momma goodbye and was out the door. My sister took me to the mall and bought me any and everything I laid my eyes on she was awesome like that.

It seemed every month she got this mysterious check in the mail with a no return address for the amount of 2 grand. Each month she helped out with bills, food and whatever else was needed in the household. She had reason to believe they came from her nonexistent father that she never met. "Hey, how about we grab something to eat...?" for my sister to eat any and everything she sure kept a tight figure. I mean she was all breast and ass; she was all of 5'11" and weighed a solid 165lbs. She was what people called a redbone but she wasn't conceited she was just overly confident.

When we got home I retired to my bedroom and on my nightstand like a neon light there was Tariq's number I picked it up and stared at it, what the hell...? I picked up my phone and dialed the number before I lost my nerve. The phone was ringing and I was nervous as hell, three rings in and right when I was about to give up and hang up I heard "Hello" I damn near dropped the phone at the sound of his deep baritone voice in my ear "May I please speak to Tariq...?" and in return he said "This is he, who's speaking...?" I lost my tongue for a minute "Umm, this is Mar

'Shaye', u know from the other night" stupid, stupid, stupid, why did I just say that like there were 50 million Mar'Shaye's in the world. "I remember you, you're the girl with the green eyes and I also remember that awesome thing you do with your backside" Tariq replied.

I was floored and humored so I just broke out in laughter. "What's so funny, I hope not me" he asked "No, It's not you it's just that...Oh what the hell" I couldn't get my thoughts from my brain to mouth for nothing in the world "Well, since you find me so amusing maybe I shouldn't waste my time or yours" he replied. "Wait, wait, wait.....OK I'm sorry, I didn't mean to offend you in any-" he cut me off and said "Stop right there you didn't offend me I was just having some fun of my own". Now here I was looking stupid glad he couldn't see my face. "Okay, let's start over, how about I take you out for dinner and then maybe we can take a walk along the Pier...?" I finally took a breath and said "Sure, Umm let me give you my address and I'll see you at 7:00...?" I crossed my fingers and waited "Sure, I can do that 7:00 p.m. it is...Bye for now Love" I couldn't breathe again so when I said my goodbye it came out all seductive like.

I ran into my sister room full of excitement and full of questions "What should I wear, how should I wear my hair, up or down....? OMG, what should I do...? I have no idea" Tanesha looked at me and with a gut wrenching laugh said "What are you yapping about calm down and start at the beginning" So I took a breath and said "Tariq, he asked me out tonight he's supposed to come pick me up at seven and

I have no idea what to wear" she looked at me with a smirk and said "Okay we can fix this, you have like three hours so I got you, hold on...Ma! Could you please come here for a second please...?" Momma came rushing in all frantic I guess it was from the way Tanesha was yelling as if the house was ablaze.

"What is it child, what's wrong now...?" Tanesha just waved her off and said "Ma, Shaye' has a date tonight with one fine, delicious piece of chocolate and she has no clue what to wear. Me personally thinks she should wear her bikini top and those awesome apple bottoms jeans that make her ass look phat and u already know she's not having it" I saw her wink in mom's direction and she then smiled and looked at me and said "Baby whatever you wear will be fine

because your simply beautiful in and out. He knows this otherwise he wouldn't be taking you out" and with that momma turned to leave before throwing over her shoulder "The red polka dot bikini top, her red Dereon Capri's and her white stilettos" she laughed and left. I looked at my sister and said "Now you got momma in on it....Help me please....I'll never ask you for anything else...I promise" I begged and she laughed and said "Yea right, we'll be right back at it again tomorrow and the next day after. Now let's go raid your closet..."

Chapter 4

My sister hooked me up she had my hair in Shirley Temple curls long and flowing. I had yet another mid-riff top on and some Coogi jeans with my Burgundy boots to match the letters across my breast and sooner rather than later I was ready by seven. I was ready and looking edible when Tariq showed up. When the doorbell rang I was beat to the door not only by Tanesha but momma as well.

Momma opened the door and said "Why don't you come in for a second Shaye' is just finishing up, she'll be down in a minute" as Tariq walked in Tanesha went further into the living room and said "Hi, Tariq" and then she walked into the kitchen with all her ass jiggling in those damn boy shorts. I was gone kill her dead when I got back home for that move alone.

As I was coming downstairs I noticed I forgot my phone so I went back to retrieve it when I heard momma say "So you met Mar 'Shaye' at the club the other night huh....?" he simply smiled and said "Yes, Ma'am" she smiled and said "Son, what do you do for a living...?" he smiled and I knew I had to hurry up so I could save him from interrogation.

When I finally made it down the stairs I noticed momma looking at Tariq kind of weird and I wondered what could of happened that quick "Momma you okay, you look a little flushed. You need some water or something...?" of course knowing momma she said "No baby, you go on and have fun...Nice to have met you Tariq" I kissed momma on the cheek and turned to Tariq and said "Let's Go, Bye Tanesha!" I yelled over my shoulder. "Bye Hooker,

Don't do nothing I would love to do" I pushed Tariq out the door in a hurry before somebody else said something stupid.

Tariq ended up doing exactly what he said he would do and took me to the movies and he let me pick the movie and of course I picked a movie that I thought would get me close to his flesh so we watched "The Devil" shit, I was terrified in that theater. I was so close to Tariq it's a wonder he could breathe at all I was damn near in his lap.

We ended up walking along the Pier after the movie and then my stomach begin to growl and Tariq looked at me and smiled and said "All you had to do was tell me you were hungry" I looked at him and smiled. We walked the short distance and had burgers at the Be-Bop Cafe' where we listened to the live musicians play random jazz tunes. I don't know how many piña colada's I had but my cousin kept bringing them being he worked there shit I was to tipsy. I was feeling nice when Tariq leaned down and whispered "You ready for me to take you home yet....?" I wanted to say no but I knew momma was up waiting as usual so I said "unfortunately yes, I don't wanna keep momma waiting. Plus, I wanna tell Tanesha all the juicy details about our date," I smiled up at him and noticed his deep dimples when he smiled down at me. "Well, tell her this also," and he raised my chin with his finger and he planted a soft sensual kiss on my lips. I loved every minute of it I didn't wanna come up for air. Once the kiss was done and all out of breath I said "Woo, which way is the car...?" he smiled and said

"This way love" I let him led the way while I thought of things to come.

When I got home momma was up and so was Tanesha Lord knows I thought she was out somewhere but there she was with a big ass bowl of popcorn watching love & basketball. I turned to Tariq and said "Thanks for walking me to the door, I really enjoyed my evening" he smiled and in return said "Me to-you know enjoyed my evening. Good Night Love," and he bent down to give me a kiss good night but I stopped him and said "Not in front of momma" I giggled I was so 18-he smiled and said "Till Next Time" and he turned and left.

I closed the door and before I could get upstairs momma said "Shaye', there's something about that boy that don't sit right with me" I looked at her and before I could get a question out edge wise Tanesha spoke up and said "What is it momma..? Is it his age..? Or is there something else juicy you want to share...?" momma gave me a sideways glance and she looked at Tanesha and then she stood and walked to her bedroom. She stopped and looked over her shoulder and said "Maybe it's just me, I don't know...it just don't feel right is all I'm saying" and with that being said she went in her room and closed the door.

Chapter 5

I went upstairs to change and I kept pondering what momma said but I couldn't put 2 and 2 together to make four. I couldn't give it much thought though because Tariq was on my mind and I needed to tell Tanesha about our date. On my way to my bedroom door it just flew open its good thing I wasn't standing behind it.

Tanesha waltz in dressed in a night gown, slippers and that stupid scarf tied around her flowing locks. "So, how was the date I want everything, leave no rock un-turned" she smiled. I looked at her sitting on my bed with her legs crossed Indian style and shook my head and joined her. I told her everything about how we went to the movies and then dinner and then a long romantic walk along the Pier holding hands and talking about nothing in particular. Tanesha sat there with her mouth open with a look of disappointment on her face and then she spoke "That's it; I stayed home for that....? Please!!! Tell me that's not it" I smiled and said "Tariq did want me to share something with you" she gave me the okay look and said "Well hell spill it already, damn."

I leaned forward and told her all dreamy like "He kissed me right before we left the Pier. The water was shimmering and the moon was full and he looked me the eyes as he titled my chin upward and then he planted one on me" I squealed with delight and so did my overly excited sister then she stopped and said "So, why didn't you let him kiss you when he dropped you off...?" I looked at her like Duh! And said "Momma was sitting there and I just didn't-I don't know, I just didn't feel right with momma as one of my audience members" Tanesha smacked her lips and said "You suck big time, "she laughed at herself and left me sitting there thinking of Tariq's lips pressed against mine. Damn, I had it bad.....

I woke up that next morning to the ringing of my phone I rolled over and picked it up not thinking to clear my throat so I ended up sounding like a man "Hello," whoever it was must of been confused because they simply said "Umm, can I please speak to Mar 'Shaye'...?" I tried clearing my throat then it went all scratchy "This is she," I finally cleared my throat when he spoke "Umm, Mar 'Shaye' I know you probably don't remember me but Umm," I was getting frustrated now and I was just about to hang up when he said

"Umm, Mar 'Shaye' this is hard for me but here goes: This is Marquise Robinson" I damn near dropped the phone when he finished with "This is your father" I couldn't get a word out edge wise I just jumped up and ran into my sister's room. I snatched Tanesha up out the bed and literally drug her to my bedroom.

Tanesha looked at me with the look of a mad woman and said "What the hell Shaye'" I couldn't get my words together so I just pointed at the phone. Tanesha looked at me then the phone and said "What the hell is wrong with you...? Is someone on the phone fuckin with you....? I looked at her as tears welled up in my eyes. She threw her hand up and stomped over to the phone and snatched it up off the floor and said "Look asshole, leave my sister alone" and she waited patiently then she looked at me and said "No one's there, who in the hell were you just talking to...?" I finally let the tears fall, Tanesha hung up the phone and walk over and wrapped her arms around me. "Shaye' your shaking, what the hell just happened...?" I cried into her chest and said "That was my father" Tanesha let me go and fell back on the bed and she looked at me "What did he say...?" I shrugged my shoulders and said "I just told you what he said that's why I came and got you" Tanesha looked at me and shook her head "Whatever you do we can't tell momma" I looked at her puzzled and said "Why, Why can't we tell momma...?" she just shook her head and said "Momma is going thru enough as it is and I just think we need to keep this to ourselves is all" I wasn't ' for sure about this one. Tanesha looked at me and said "Please Shaye' promise me this one thing...?" I looked at my sister and I gave in and said "I promise" she got up and left with her feet dragging and left me exhausted with no options. I brushed my teeth, combed my hair and threw on some clothes and went down for breakfast.

Chapter 6

I joined momma and Tanesha at the breakfast nook and they were having a discussion about my birthday coming up in a few weeks. I wanted to join in but my mind was still on my father calling this morning. Momma placed my breakfast in front of me and said "Hey Baby, Are you feeling okay this morning..? You look a little flustered" I smiled and looked at momma and said No momma, I'm not flustered I do have a question though" Tanesha looked at me like she would kill me later but I blew it off.

Momma looked at me sideways and said "Shoot" I cleared my throat and said "What is it about Tariq that doesn't sit right with you...? You never did tell me" Tanesha finally was able to breath and she then looked at momma for her answer.

Momma looked at me and said "Shaye' to be honest with you his eyes look so familiar. I promise you I've seen those eyes before I just don't know where, It's a little unsettling" I shook my head and said "His eyes momma, really...?" she shook her head and said under her breath "it's something familiar about that's boy's eyes" and she walked into her bedroom and closed the door. I looked at Tanesha and said "Well that was strange" she looked at me and said "Yea, that was kind of strange but you know momma....she thinks she knows everybody" and she looked at me and smiled.

I put my plate in the kitchen sink. I looked at Tanesha and walked into the living room and grabbed my keys to my BMW Bug and proceeded out the door. I needed some much needed air to clear my head. While I was riding thru the hood I picked up my phone and dialed Tariq "Hey You, How would you like to meet me down by the water. I'm at the 31st street beach" he quickly agreed and said he was on his way. As I was sitting on the rocks with my knees drawn to my chest starring out at the water I felt a hand touch my shoulder. I smiled up at Tariq has his beautiful grey eyes sparkled in the sunlight. "Hey you, thanks for coming" he looked at me kind of strange and said "What's wrong Love, you look kind of upset about something" I just shrugged my shoulders and said "Have a seat Tariq and let me get to know you" so he sat down beside me and said "Where do I start...?" I tried smiling but it failed me and I said "Why not start at the beginning Please.....!"

Chapter 7

"Okay umm, where to start, I was born an addict July 15, 1989 to a Marie Gonzalez. I was raised in a single parent dwelling in hot ass Phoenix Arizona. My momma worked sometimes two jobs to make sure I have everything I needed. I was seven years of age when my mom relapsed to her boyfriend at the time. She lost one job but she tried her damnest to hold on to the second with no avail. She ended up on welfare and that angered her but it was like she didn't care one way or another.

We were put out the street some years later for the simple fact and reason momma would move to have a roof over our heads but then she wouldn't pay the rent. The landlord came up stairs one day I think I was ten at the time and he told momma rent was due and she was behind three months. Momma then packed us up and we were back out on the street. We stayed in abandon building and we slept in abandoned cars. Sometimes we had to fight over were to sleep because of the other homeless people. I was able to bathe and go to school during the week due to this one old lady that felt sorry for my situation. She sometimes feed me and made sure I had clothes and sometime shoes but momma would always yell at her. She would always say "We don't need your help" in my eyes we needed all the help we could get.

She would sometimes go to the grocery store and steal food and candles so that way I could do my homework. She would sell her body so I could have clean school clothes during the week. We finally got stable enough to have a roof over our heads due to another boyfriend I was now twelve. He would come over and have sex with my mother and give her, her fix and then he would leave and we wouldn't see him until the next day.

I would sit in front of the TV and listen to my mother in the other room crying and screaming. I never knew what she was going thru but she always came out the room with a smile on her face and fresh scratches on her arm. She would scratch her head, then her arms and say "Baby you hungry" I would look at her and say "No Ma'am" and she would sit down in the kitchen chair and basically fall asleep with her chin touching her chest.

My birthday finally approached and I wanted so badly for momma to be sober at least an hour at least she could do was give me an hour. I woke up that morning brushed my teeth, washed my face, and found me an outfit that wasn't reeking of last week's funk. My clothes hadn't been washed in weeks due to her and Junior constantly being locked up in that room. I think he was smoking his own product to be honest.

Anyway, I got dressed and went into the living room and there was momma sitting in her chair nodding off with her head in her chest. I walked over and said "Bye Momma," I kissed her forehead and went out the door to school. I had never met my father until this very day. The last bell had just rung and I was debating on whether I should go home or not when a nice Lincoln Town car pulled up and this man climbed out wearing a three piece suit he was all of 6'6" and he had my eyes and *he was all of 240lbs at least. When he approached me he introduced himself and I was still kind of wary until he told me he was my father. He asked if I wanted to take a ride with him and I climbed in still feeling a little skeptical. All the kids that bullied me and talked about me were thrown for a loop and that was the best part.*

He took me to get something to eat and we talked about why he left and why was he just coming back. He talked around the subject and I was just about fed up "Look Dad, I'm ready to go home....Momma is gonna be worried about me" I stood up and then he said "Sit down son, there's something we must discuss. It's about your mother," I sat down and looked at this man and thought what now.

My dad cleared his throat and hung his head and said "Son, your mother passed away this morning from a drug overdose," he then looked me square in the eyes and said "I'm sorry son." I held my head down and cried. That was the day my new life begin, I missed momma like you wouldn't believe but I made a promise to myself to make her proud. I hopped on a plane and moved to Manhattan New York where I graduated from high school with honors.

I soon left New York and headed back to my old stomping ground the Windy City this is where I went to college and received my Juris Doctorate for me to become a criminal lawyer. Now here I am an intern at Andrew M. Weisberg and that's my life in a nut shell"

Chapter 8

Well damn here I was fresh out of high school and my life was just beginning and it was easy breezy compared to his life. "So you're like 22 and you're already a lawyer...?" I knew it was stupid but that was all I had. "Yea, I guess you can say that but I'm still an intern" he smiled. He looked at me as if he was concerned and said "So Mar 'Shaye' how did such a beautiful woman like yourself end up here today...?" I cleared my throat and I begin my uninteresting life story "As you already know my name is Mar 'Shaye' Vines and I was born July 30, 1993. I wasn't born an addict not to point fingers or anything but I was also raised by my mom.

See, my dad left when I was like eight years old and he never looked back. He told momma that he had dreams to pursue or something like that so he packed up and moved to Brooklyn, New York. Momma spent all her time working sometimes two and three jobs to make sure the bills and the house note was paid and of course she had me to take care of. Sure I had all the necessities a little girl could possibly want but I didn't see momma as often as I wanted.

My dad would send me birthday cards and an occasional Christmas gift but it wasn't the same anymore. Then I remember one day momma being off from work and we were sitting in the living room watching TV when we heard the tiniest knock on the door and when she went to open it there stood Tanesha. She was standing there cold with no shoes on her feet, her hair was a mess and she had all her clothes in shopping bags and she had a note attached to her jacket. I remember momma shooing me upstairs to take my bath for bed as she brought this stranger into our house. So a lady from Oklahoma decided to drive the allotted hours to Chicago just to drop her off on momma's stoop.

After momma interrogated the poor child she fed her, bathed her, and sent her off to bed. We never knew what was in that note but momma stayed up the whole night crying and yelling at no one in particular. That morning at breakfast momma introduced us and said that from now on we would remain sisters and no one was allowed to break that bond. No matter how much we fight, argue, and scream our heads off no one can't tell me that Tanesha is not my biological sister. Anyway, today I got a phone call from the man that walked off and left me ten years ago. I was a bit shaken up when he mentioned who he was so I dropped the phone and ran. I snatched my sister up and when she picked up the phone he was gone. I wanted to tell momma but Tanesha thought it was better not to say anything.

I normally tell momma everything and this one is kind of hard to keep to myself. It's kind of hard trying to figure out what he wants after all these years. Maybe he's feeling guilty about not being there for my graduation or any of my accomplishments for that matter. So, here we are out at the Lake soul searching" I looked in his eyes and thought about momma and threw it off.

Tariq looked at me and said "Wow, you hungry because I'm starved" I looked at him and I couldn't control my laughter and said "Sure," we ended up getting Italian Beefs on the move. We walked along the beach and talked. Sooner rather than later we ended up downtown in the lion's den at Brookfield Zoo making out. I went back to Tariq's place if I could call it that he lived in this beautiful high-rise right smack in the middle of the downtown area.

The living room opened up into the kitchen area. The living room was made up in earth tones with a lot of African mask and art sculptures. I went into the kitchen and everything was a bright white and all the appliances were a stainless steel. I didn't venture pass that point without Tariq's approval.

Tariq was looking at me with a mischievous smirk and then he said "You want the tour of the bachelor pad...?" I smirked back and said "Sure, Now I ain't gone find nobody's left over perfume or underwear am I..." he laughed and took my hand in his "Since you've seen the living room and kitchen, how about we take a tour of the bedroom" I smiled and followed closely behind him down this long hallway. I passed a total of three doors that I assumed I would see later hopefully.

I walked into his bedroom and I was in total awe his room was done up in black and white. His bed alone was made for twelve I think that's what they called a California King. The comforters on the bed I fell in love with: It was an all-white comforter set with a big ying yang symbol dead in the center. He laid back on the bed and said "Go be nosy, I know you want to and no, you will not find any leftover *underwear, I promise" I looked at him and said "Yea OK, Let me find out" and he laughed his ass off. I looked at him and said "I ain't laughing," he had a Jacuzzi tub, big enough for six at least. In one corner alone stood a huge shower stall with nuzzles in every nook and cranny.*

I loved the huge shower head in the center of the shower, turning it on would feel like a rain shower. His sink was done up in black and white as well he had the whole double sink thing happening but the sink itself was glass bowls. I was finally headed towards the exit when I noticed a door which I thought was the linen closet but when I opened it there stood the toilet and a plasma screen TV on the wall.

There was a mini magazine rack by the toilet and of a remote for the TV I guess. This was too much all I could do was shake my head and close the door. In doing so I finally looked down at the floor and of course it was white but the very center was another ying yang symbol.

Once out the bathroom I laid down on the bed beside Tariq and he said "So the highlight of the evening is" and he stood up and walked to the patio doors he turned and said "Would you mind standing by my side Ms. Vines" I scooted out the bed and walked over to stand beside him. He looked at me and said "Now close your eyes and on the count of three open them" I shook my head and closed my eyes.

I heard the drapes slide back and I heard the traffic flow in and then I heard the countdown. I felt him wrap his arms around me and I felt the wind on my face. When he got to three I was flabbergasted and terrified here I was up on the 30th floor of a high-rise looking at the most beautiful view ever. Tariq kissed my neck and said "I want this moment right here, right now to be our moment" I turned around and threw my arms around Tariq's neck and kissed him with all I had to offer. He pulled me close and pressed his body to mine and I enjoyed every minute of it.

We soon ended up back on the bed where I stretched out and allowed him to kiss me from my neck to my navel "Wait Tariq," he paused "Yes Mar 'Shaye'," I cleared my throat and took a breath and said "Tariq, this is hard for me but Umm, imma virgin" Tariq looked at me and said "Wow, Umm, that's cool" he crawled up on the bed "Is it okay for me to hold you" I smiled and said "Sure" and that night for me was the most romantic. Tariq held me close to the sound of downtown traffic and a cool breeze.

Chapter 9

I arrived home around one that morning and momma wasn't waiting up as usual and Tanesha was nowhere to be found. I kissed Tariq good night and headed up to bed to get some rest. That morning I woke up to momma sitting in my bedroom in my rocking chair by the window. "Momma what's the matter...?" she kept on rocking in that chair as if she didn't hear me. "Momma...?" she stops rocking long enough to look over her shoulder at me and then she begins rocking again. I got up and went into the bathroom and washed my face and brushed my teeth.

When I came out the bathroom there was a box sitting in the middle of my bed I approached it like it was liquid fire. "Momma what's this...?" she continued to rock and she said over her shoulder "Just open it" I was terrified momma was acting strange and she never acted this way. I sat down on the bed and right when I was about to open the box my door sprang open and in ran Tanesha "Shaye' come quick, hurry up" I jumped off the bed and momma stopped rocking in that rocker and we all ran down stairs.

Monet was downstairs crying her eyes out "Monet what's wrong....?" she looked up still crying and said "Its momma, I just found out she has cancer" we all looked like deer caught in headlights. "Monet, I'm so sorry" I sat down beside her and she rested her head on my shoulder and cried harder. Tanesha went into the kitchen and came back with a tall glass of ice tea and momma sat down on in her recliner and started to pray and I mean she prayed.

After sitting up with Monet for hours on end she finally went home momma told her she could stay if she wanted but she refused. Tanesha and I sat up and watched TV for a couple of hours and then I went upstairs to my bedroom and the closer I got the more I was anxious to find out what was in that box but once there the box was gone. I headed back downstairs to ask momma about the box but she was asleep so I left it alone until tomorrow.

I went back upstairs and got ready for bed and as soon as my head hit the pillow my phone rung "Hello," I knew someone was there because I could hear them breathing "Hello," then I heard music in the background I think it was Luther Vandross "Hey Love," I smiled and *said "Hi Tariq" he then said "What you doing tomorrow...?" I smiled and said "Nothing special, Why...?" he cleared his throat and said "I wanna take you dancing tomorrow nite if you don't mind...?" I then recognized the song and started to sing along "Excuse me miss....But what's your name...?...Where are you from and I can come...?...And possibly can I take you out tonite" and then he started in "To a movie...to the park....I'll have you home before it's dark...So let me know, can I take you out tonite....?" I began to laugh "yea, that's fine we can go dancing tomorrow....what time should I be ready...?" he cleared his throat and said "How about 8...Is that cool...?" I had to be sarcastic "But I thought you said you'll have me home before its dark...?" he laughed and said "Bye Love, Tomorrow at 8...?" I smiled and responded with "Bye*

Tariq, 8 it is" and then he hung up. I heard Tanesha coming up the stairs she stopped and knocked before coming in and said "Good Nite Shaye'" I smiled "Good Nite Nesha" and she closed the door and went to her bedroom.

I laid there thinking not only of Tariq and our date tomorrow but also on how to tell momma about daddy calling. She has been acting really strange lately and I'm still curious as to what's in that box....

Chapter 10

That morning I awoke to the sound of my phone ringing I cleared my throat "Hello," I heard traffic noise so I thought it was Tariq. "Hello," there was a horn blowing then I heard "Hello, may I please speak to Mar 'Shaye'...?" I sat up in bed and said "This is she, who's calling...?" I heard another horn blow and someone yelling at the top of their lungs. "Umm, this is your father calling" I took a deep breathe "Hi Daddy, How are you..?" I guess he was thrown off his square when he said "Umm, Wow....Umm, I know we have a lot to discuss and I was wondering if we can do it this weekend. I'll be in town on business" I sighed with anticipation "OK, where we will have this discussion...?" I heard him talking to someone and then he said "How about we meet downtown by the Pier...?" I thought about it and said "How about not, How about you come to the house...? I don't wanna hide you from momma she has a right to know what is going on. So, how does that work for you...? He cleared his throat and said "OK, I'll stop by this weekend," I took a much needed breathe and said "OK Daddy, I'll see you this weekend....Bye" he said his good byes and then we hung up.

I crawled out of bed and went into Tanesha's room and laid down on the bed beside her and said "Tanesha, Daddy will be here this weekend and I need your support. I know this is difficult for you, you not knowing your father and all but I need you there with me so I can steal your energy" she smiled at me and said "Sure thing Shaye' and when I see him momma *better had got to him first because I might just slap him stupid. I have no idea why he even left in the first place and momma is beautiful. If it hadn't been for momma and of course you accepting me as a part of the family. Where would I be....?" I placed my head up against hers and we laid there and talked about nothing.*

Then I remembered that I had a date tonite "Nesha, I'm gonna need you to hook up my hair for tonight, I'm going dancing" she shoved me out the bed onto the floor and said "I thought you said you wouldn't bug me no more skank" then she smiled and said "Sure," I bounced off the floor onto the bed and tickled Nesha until she was gasping for air. The door swung open and there stood momma "What y'all doing in here..." we both laughed and said "Nothing" she smiled and said "Breakfast in 10 minutes" we both looked at each other and broke out in laughter. Momma went to close the door and I said "Momma there is something we need to discuss sometime today before you get to busy" she shook her head and closed the door.

We went down to breakfast and sat down with momma and talked about my birthday coming up and when I mention Tariq she would clam up and become distant. Tanesha went upstairs to take a shower. She said something about going out tonite with this dude she just met I just hope she did my hair before she left and I think I needed a new outfit and fresh pair of heels.

Momma was washing dishes "Momma come sit down for a moment" she wiped her hands on her apron and then came and sat down across from me

"Momma I have some things to discuss with you and I don't think you're gonna like it" Momma then got up and went into the fridge and grabbed the apple juice and two glasses. "Momma come sit down I'm trying to talk to you..." she looked at me and came back to the table "Momma I need-" I was rudely interrupted "Is this about that boy...? What's his name again...?" I shook my head and said "No momma and his name is Tariq" she threw her hands up "Look if your finna tell me something about this boy then I don't wanna here it" I was getting frustrated "MOMMA LISTEN TO ME!!!!" she snapped her head up "Don't you holler at me in my house ever, do you understand me..? I could feel the tears building "Momma I sorry but this is about the phone call-" I was interrupted by the doorbell "DAMMIT!!!"

I got up to answer the door and in walked Shanei' loud and in charge "Girl, you going to the mall with us or what...? And then Tanesha came down the stairs looking fierce "Yea Shaye' you should come" I shook my head no "I'm trying to talk to momma about something really important" momma rounded the corner and said "You gone head and go with your sister we can talk about this later. Whatever it may be..." she then turned and went into her bedroom.

I went upstairs and threw on a pair of jeans and some tennis shoes. I snatched up my purse, keys and of course my cell and headed down stairs and out the door.

Chapter 11

I went shopping with my sister and loud ass Shanei' and believe you me she hit on everybody imaginable male and female she had no shame in her game at all. We went to Macy's and I picked up some shoes and then we headed over to Victoria's Secret and I bought me some more pantie and bra sets. Shanei' asked me if I was getting all dolled up for Tariq and I told her of course. She got a laugh out of that one.

"How long have you guys been going out now...?" I thought about it and we've been together for a moth now and I was excited to call him my Boo. Shanei' look at me and said what was on her mind "You plan on losing your virginity aren't you...?" I just smiled and looked down at my feet. "You whore, I knew you had it in

you somewhere...at least you would like to" I looked at her disgusted "You know what Shanei' your ass is nasty..." Tanesha came around the corner and said "What her hoe ass say now...?" I laughed and said "Nothing" Shanei' coughed into her fist and mumbled something under her breath. She then turned to Tanesha and said "Your whore of a sister is planning on losing her virginity to that fine ass Tariq" Tanesha's mouth fell open and then she came in closer to me "Are you sure Shaye'...?" I looked at her and said "I think he's special Nesha and I really like him. Hell, I might even love him do you know the other nite when he found out I was a virgin he backed up. He looked at me and asked if it was okay for him to hold me and I just loved it. He didn't turn tail and run or try to force sex on me like some of my previous boyfriends. I really do like him

Nesha..." My sister looked at me and said "Bitch you got it bad..." we then paid for our things and sat down in the food court and ate and talked about both our dates tonight. Shanei' sat there sucking her teeth the whole time talking about "It Must Be Nice" we both looked at her and said "Hater," and then we all burst out in laughter.

We arrived home at about 6:30 that evening I ran my things upstairs and threw them on the bed and ran back down stairs to catch momma before she left for work "Momma can you spare 5 minutes before you leave...?" Momma then smacked her lips like I was getting on her nerves. "Momma what is this attitude...? You've been acting strange for the pass month. Does me seeing Tariq upset you or something...? What is it about him *momma...? Why is it all of a sudden you try to avoid me at all cost...? Every time I open my mouth you get all fidgety. What is it momma...? she looked at me and continued to button her jacket she looked up and said "We'll talk about this in the morning, right now I need to go to work.." she then turned to reach for the door knob when I said "Daddy called momma and he'll be here this weekend" she spun around and slapped my face.*

That hadn't happen in years, what did I do to deserve that. I looked at momma with tears in my eyes and asked "Why momma...? What did I do...?" she looked at me fuming and asked "How dare he call my house and talk to anyone...? Mistake #1 and #2 how dare you call him daddy...? I did this; I sacrificed for you and your sister. As far as your daddy is concerned he's dead to me now. Do you her me Shaye'.....DEAD!!!!...." and she slammed out the door.

When I turned around there stood Tanesha. Tanesha stretched her arms out to me and I ran into them and cried. Tanesha then rubbed my hair back and said "Let's get you ready for Tariq" we headed upstairs and I was fierce by the time the doorbell rung at 5 minutes till 8.

Tanesha ran down the stairs to get the door "What up Tariq, My sister should be down in a minute. If you want you can have a seat in the dining room" I heard him asking Nesha where was momma and I heard her say "She had to work tonight, just so happens she has one of those jobs that call when they need you and not the other way round. I wish I didn't have to go to work every day of the week" she laughed then I heard her running up the stairs. "So Nesha, here goes...tomorrow when I see you I'll be a woman" my sister laughed at me and asked "You got everything...?" I went thru my over nite bag and said "Yea, I got everything....I then kissed her on the cheek and headed towards the stairs when I heard the front door fly open.

I looked at Tanesha and we both said "Momma" I went for the stairs and I heard "Get your shit and get the fuck outta my house" I heard Tariq say "Excuse Me...?" I heard momma say "If you don't get up and get the fuck out right now I promise you I will call the police on you for trespassing" I finally made it down the stairs with Tanesha on my heels. "Ma'am I have no idea what's going on here...What have I done...? I've been with your daughter for a *month now and you seemed fine with that...So, what's with the change...?" Momma then went into her room and I knew she was going to get Nina that's what she called her gun. "Tariq let's go" he looked at me puzzled I pulled on his arm and said "Now Tariq, " Nesha snatched the door open and said "Go, I'll handle momma"*

I was half way out the door when momma rounded the corner "Where do you think you going...?" I looked at her and said "Please momma don't do this," she looked at me and said "Gone, Gone head....I can't stop you, you grown..." she walked up on me and I thought I was slapped again "Get out my doorway Shaye' come back when you got some sense..." she then shoved me and slammed the door in my face. I went to the car defeated. "What was all that about...?" Tariq asked "I guess this means were not going dancing...?" I laughed through the tears. "Hey Love, if that's what you wanna do then I'm game but I think you need a hot bath and a nice back rub" I looked up at him thru my tears and asked "And where do I get this treatment...?" He smiled and pulled off. I let my seat back and let the ride consume me. I had at least 45 minutes to think before we reached the city.

Chapter 12

I arrived in the city and the lights were beautiful. Tariq pulled into the underground garage and then we caught the elevator up to the 30th floor. Once Tariq opened the doors I headed straight for the couch I was worn out and I hadn't done anything yet. Tariq placed my bag by the couch and he went into the kitchen and came out with two glasses and some bottled water. "If you want something stronger let me know..." I looked at him and said "What do you have..?" he went thru the list and came up with: Cabernet, Merlot, Chardonnay, Pinot Noir, Sauvignon Blanc, Pinot Grigio, and Zinfandel.

Then he took a breath and recited the other list: Brandy, Vodka, Gin, Rum and Tequila. I looked at him and said "How about a nice wine...You pick" he came back into the living room with a bottle of Chardonnay he poured me my first glass and set the remainder on the table. He looked at me and said "I'll be right back I need to check my messages" I sat there and relaxed my mind. I couldn't wrap my mind around the reason momma was tripping so hard. It wasn't like Tariq mistreated me in any way he was always a gentleman. I just couldn't understand it; I wish I had opened that damn box maybe that holds the answer to this mess.

Tariq reappeared and took me by the hand and led me to the bedroom. Where the patio doors were open and the covers were pulled back on the bed and on the bed lie a t-shirt and some ankle socks. There beside that lay a towel and some toiletries. "I ran you a bath and I went out the other day and bought you some toiletries. I had no idea when this day would happen but I wanted to be prepared. I guess this day came sooner than I thought" he smiled. I sat down at the foot of the bed to pull off my shoes and he rushed right over "Let me do that for you" as he pulled off each shoe he massaged my feet and then once he was done he asked me to stand.

As I stood there bold and unsure he unzipped my dress from the side and said "Hold your arms up Boo, let me undress you" I placed my hands high above my head and he raised my dress up slightly and he then rubbed his hands along my hips and in doing so I let out a slight moan. I was a little tipsy but that didn't stop me from appreciating his touch. He raised my dress a little higher and my 38

DD's were present and wanted to say "Hello," he placed his face between my breasts and inhaled. I let my head roll back on my neck and I moaned some more just a little louder this time. My dress was finally over my head and thrown on the bed and I looked up at him hungrily and I wanted him right then and there so I reached out to kiss his lips and he obliged. I ran my hands along the back of his neck and pulled him closer so I could get a deeper more passionate kiss and he gave in to me.

When we came up for air I was looking up at him with wanting and he was looking down at me with the expression of love. I raised my voice slightly and said "Make Love to Me Tariq" he cleared his throat and said "Are you sure My Love," I looked at him and this was the first in a long time I was ever sure about something. So I looked up at him and I met him eye to eye and said "Yes, I'm very sure" he started in with a soft gentle kiss at first but the longer it lasted the more the passion was evident then and only then I knew what it was like to be sexually aroused. I could feel my panties becoming moist with anticipation. Tariq unhooked my lace front bra and my 38 DD's sprang free.

He placed one in each hand and kissed each nipple as if they were fragile. He placed each nipple between his lips and suckled as if a new born after his mother's milk. This was feeling too good so I allowed myself to relax and let him have his way. Tariq stretched me out on the bed and he kissed my lips then my neck and I moaned with pleasure. He flicked his tongue over each nipple and then ran his tongue further down to my navel. I became nervous all over again and then I heard him speak softly "Relax My Love, I won't hurt you I promise" so I relaxed because I believed him. He ran his fingers along my pantie line and went to remove my thong and I raised my hips and allowed him access.

He rose up just enough to place my legs in his grasp and he began to kiss my thighs. This was heaven sent I couldn't maintain my trembling body any longer. I felt his cool breath on my concha and I begged him to proceed. He placed one finger at my door and he pushed and I trembled. He pushed again and I trembled: "Relax" I took two deep breaths and tried to calm my nerves. "If I'm hurting you let me know..." I shook my head up and down and tried to concentrate on other things besides the pain like the pleasure. I felt him place his thumb on my clit and he began to rub in clockwise circles and my legs began to tremble. I cried out in ecstasy "Tariq.....OMG" he sped up the pace just a little and I let my mind go blank and then and only then was I to get pass the pain and enjoy the pleasure. "Am I hurting you...?" I tried talking but this was lovely "Tariq, I'm.....Ohhhh, Shit" I felt him pushing with one finger and twirling with the other and then my body began to shake and my back arched into a perfect C.

I remember clamping my legs in around his head and yelling at the top of my lungs "TARIQ, I'M CUMMIN..." I was trying to get away when he started milking me for everything I had to offer "Tariq, Please....(Panting)　　Stop....(Panting)

Ohhhh, Shit...(Panting)Tariq...(Panting) Damn U....(Panting)" he finally stopped and came up for air and as he crawled up the length of body I was on cloud nine singing back up for Patti Labelle. "Are you alright My Love," all I could manage at the time was a smile and a head nod due to my body still trembling and a loss of oxygen.

Tariq stood up and pulled his wife beater over his head and what a chiseled mess he was there was muscles everywhere. It was as if God was a woman and made this man all for herself but somehow he escaped. He then removed his sweats and his dick was swollen I mean I could easily see that he was carrying at least an eight or nine inch. My nerves returned because the whole time I was thinking is this really about to happen...?

Oh, Wow.....He's gonna kill me with all he's packing...I just couldn't get over my nerves until his boxers were off and his dick sprang free. He then laid down beside me and asked "Are you sure about this...?" I smiled and I ran my hand along his prized possession and said "I'm sure" and with a kiss it was on.

Chapter13

I woke up the next morning feeling sore but I had a smile on my face. When I rolled over Tariq wasn't there and I panicked. I threw Tariq's wife beater over my frame and walked out into the living room and there he stood in the kitchen wearing nothing but his boxers.

I walked up behind him and wrapped my arms around his waist and placed my head in the crease of his back. "Good Morning Love, How did you sleep...? I smiled on the inside and replied "Magnificent" and I snuggled closer. He gave my hands a light tap and I let go so he could spin around "So, are we up and ready for breakfast...?" I smiled and said "Sure, What are we having" he looked down at me and said "Stuffed Waffles" I smiled and replied "That's Cool" he led me to the breakfast nook "You looking mighty fine in that wife beater...Ms. Vines" I looked over my shoulder at him and said "You don't look so bad either Mr. Gonzalez wearing them boxer briefs like you do" we both shared a laugh then we sat down to eat.

Tariq had to go into work later that day to prep a case for one of the top lawyers in the firm he told me I was more than welcome to stay if I wanted and if I need to go anywhere there was a set a keys by the door to his midnight black Monte' Carlo. "Take care of my baby now" he kissed me and he was out the door. I took a shower and threw on some clean underwear and of course the clothes from yesterday and headed out.

I ended up driving home hoping momma was there so we could talk. The *ride home helped me think about some things but I still didn't understand why she was acting this way I wish she would just tell me already. I pulled into the driveway and momma's car was missing in action.*

I saw the door swing open and out came Tanesha with her signature baseball bat "Girl, You almost ended up with a concussion and few broken body parts. Who car you sporting because I thought your man drove a Charger...?" I laughed and said "My man does drive a Charger. This is his baby he's trusting me with let him tell it" she walked over and gave me a hug "Heifer I missed you, want you come in and tell me all about last nite and I'll tell you what's going on with momma" we went into the house arm in arm "Where is momma anyway...?" Tanesha shook her head "Momma left early this morning

*saying something about working a double"
I sat at the breakfast table and Tanesha
brought me a glass of apple juice.*

*We sat in that kitchen for hours
talking about her date last night with this
new guy named Malik. Tanesha told me
that she didn't like him all that much
because he was always talking about
himself. I then told her about my night with
Tariq and about me losing my virginity
and she listen intently. "So, was it worth
the wait...?" I smiled and said "Hell Yea,"
we broke in laughter and headed upstairs
to my bedroom.*

*I grabbed my small suitcase and
started throwing some of my things inside
and Tanesha sat on my bed "What the hell
do you think you doing...?" I looked at her
and replied "I'm packing my things, I need
something to wear while I'm trying to*

figure all this out" Tanesha smacked her lips "Look Shaye' I love you dearly but please don't base what you're feeling now for Tariq around the fact that you just lost your virginity..." I looked at her "Tanesha please not you to" Tanesha folded her legs Indian style and said "Come sit with me for a minute" I stopped what I was doing and sat down beside my sister. "Look momma has been going thru a lot lately and she tends to lash out at the wrong people sometime. She's been pulling doubles on the job and she's been having a lot of chest pains lately which I don't think you noticed. Momma spent all her time trying to make sure we were taken care off but she never looked out for herself. It's up to us now to look out for momma. I have no idea why she doesn't like Tariq I really don't. I think he's a sweetheart if you ask me but momma don't wanna talk about it at least not yet, Shaye' she didn't mean what she said to you the other day she was just under a lot of stress. Please Shaye' think about this before you just pack up and leave..." I let my sister have her say then

"Look Nesha, I'm not packing up and leaving forever just a few days and then I'll be back. I want momma to cool off first and she's not gonna do that with Tariq being around every day. Nesha I love you and momma but this is my life remember and I can do with it as I please. I'll be back Nesha I promise," she looked at me with tears in her eyes and said "Will you be here when your daddy comes...?" I hadn't thought about that so I reached over and grabbed my cordless and programmed his number into my cell "I'll call him and tell him. I'll let him know

when it's cool to come visit." Tanesha wiped her tears and left me to do my packing. I hated to do this but it was my life and I had a right to live it to the fullest or die getting there.

Chapter14

I went out into the hall and yelled out to Tanesha that I was leaving she stepped out of the bathroom and gave me a hug and said "I love you Shaye' call me when you get back to the city" I hugged her with all my might "I love you Nesha and I'll do just that and when Tariq gets home I'll make sure it's cool first then I'll be giving you the address so you can come see me.." I pulled away and turned for the stairs.

By the time I got to the car I was a mess. I saw Tanesha looking out her bedroom window and my heart broke even more. I started the engine and backed out the driveway. As I was driving down the street I passed momma and since the windows were tinted she couldn't see me but I got a hell of a mean mug. I jumped on the highway and in the process I called

Tariq "Hey You, I'm on my way back into the city. You need anything before I get to the condo...?" he stopped to talk to someone then he replied "No Love, I don't need anything I got enough of what I need when I get home" I had to ask "And what's that..?" he cleared his throat and said "You of course" I smiled from the inside out "OK...I'll see you when you when you get home"-"Alright Love, Bye"-"Bye Tariq, I love you" Dammit did I just say that out loud. He chuckled and said "It's OK Shaye', I love you to" and we hung up and I sang all the way home.

I had been staying with Tariq for three weeks now and it was beautiful. We ate out on the patio often, every other night we walked along the Pier. We went for long drives and listened to music and sang off key. I was really falling for Tariq and I could tell the feelings were mutual. I received a phone call from my sister one nite at about 11:30 and she was hysterical "Shaye' you gotta come quick its momma..."

I jumped up outta bed and asked "Where are you..." she was breathing erratic "Where at Presbyterian Hospital" I shook Tariq "Baby wake up its momma..." he jumped up and grabbed me and him a pair of sweats and we threw on our wife beaters and grabbed our jackets at the door and headed out. Tariq had just bought him an Escalade and he was pushing the limits.

We arrived at Presbyterian in no time I ran into the emergency room and approached the nurses' station "I need to find my momma" the nurse looked at me like she didn't want to be at work that night "I need a name ma'am" she said with all attitude "Bitch don't make me..." and right when Tariq walked in my sister came thru the double doors "Shaye' she's back here, hurry up" she threw over her shoulder a hello to Tariq and we kept shit moving. "Tanesha what happened...?" I said crying. "Momma was sitting in that damn chair in the living room rubbing her chest.

I kept asking her if she was alright and she kept saying "I'm fine girl, just go get me some water" so I went into the kitchen and grabbed her a bottle of water out the fridge and I went back into the living room where she was slumped over and barely breathing. So I called the ambulance and here we stand"

Just as she was finishing up out came the Dr. "Hello, My name is Dr. Enoch" he *shook our hands and we introduced ourselves and he continued "Your mother has high blood pressure and on top of that she's just suffered a mild heart attack. My suggestion is after she leaves here which we'll give her a few days to rest but when she gets home you girls need to make sure she continues to get her rest. She's not allowed back to work for at least six weeks..." he paused and I jumped right in "Can we see her please..?" he looked at me and said "Sure, right this way" we followed Dr. Enoch to my momma's room and the way she was laying there was scary in itself but I had to be strong.*

I approached the bed "Momma...?" I could see her eyes flicker "Momma...?" her eyes sprang open and she smiled "Shaye' I've missed you" I bent down and placed my head on her chest and said "I've missed you to momma I'm so sorry about everything" she rubbed her hand across my hair and said "I know baby, I know...I'm sorry also about everything said and done" Tanesha then walked over and stood on her left side.

Momma then looked at us both and said "I love you girls so much, the both of you...there are no favorites. I love the both of you the same and if my life ends tonight let it end with you knowing that much..." she then began coughing and I passed her the cup of water that was on the nite stand and Tanesha helped her sit up and then and only then did she spot Tariq. The shit was about to hit the fan......

Chapter 15

Momma looked at Tariq and she said "What are you doing here....? Why are you here...?" I tried to convince momma it wasn't wise to get excited right after her ordeal. Tanesha tried to get her to lay down with no avail "I don't know what it is about you but your eyes are so vaguely familiar. I know you from somewhere; maybe you were one of my patients that wasn't quite right. Maybe you were one of those drug dealer thugs' boys that walk around here preying on young women. Answer me this Tariq. Where do your parents stay and what are their names...?"

I tried to get momma to lay down "Momma please not right now, let's get you better first please momma" momma shoed me away as if I was a bothersome fly. "Get out my face girl, I wanna know who this boy belong to....Answer me boy speak up...?" Momma was starting to sweat and Tanesha pushed the buzzer for the nurse. I heard the nurse over the intercom and she heard momma yelling at us to leave her alone. Tariq stood there then cleared his throat and said "Ma'am my mother passed away when I was thirteen and my father's name is-" then the door swung open and the nurse starting shooing everybody out.

"Alright, you have managed to upset the patient and it's not good in her condition. So you all must leave and I do mean now..." Since Tanesha volunteered to stay with momma overnight I kissed her forehead and told her I'll be by tomorrow to check on her. She then looked at me and said "Shaye' something ain't right about that boy" I looked at her and said

"Momma he's fine...He treats me nice and he makes sure I'm happy. Isn't that all that matters" she looked at me and shook her head from side to side and said "Yea baby it is all that matters but there's something about him and I'm trying to warn you" I kissed momma's hand and said "Momma I love you but I gotta go. I'll be by tomorrow. I promise" she then shooed me away and then whispered something to Tanesha.

Tanesha then told the nurse she'll be back she just had to make a run for momma. Once down stairs Tariq went and got the truck "Tanesha, please help me understand what's going on...?" Tanesha looked at me and said "We'll understand tomorrow when you come over. Momma asked me to go to the house and get her things and some stupid hat box. So, you'll be here tomorrow right...?" I looked at her and said "Sure, I'll be here...I have some last minute school applications to send off and then I have an interview at two o'clock so any time after that I'll be here" Tanesha gave me a hug as Tariq was pulling the car around "I love you Nesha" she then let me go and said "I love you to Shaye'...Gone head get outta here and Tariq take care of my sister" he smiled and said "You know I will" and I jumped in and we headed home.

I never did make it to the hospital the next day and Tanesha was pissed "Why in the hell aren't you here Shaye' you promised" I cleared my throat and I replied "Look Nesha I know I promised but I'm out and about and I'm trying to get these papers sent off. They changed my job interview from two o'clock to three. I have a hair appointment at four and I need to get home and cook and have dinner ready by six for Tariq when he gets home" I was driving myself crazy. "Let me ask you this, are you gonna be here when they release momma tomorrow...?" I pulled over and parked in front of the post office "What time tomorrow because I promised Tariq I wouldn't miss date night..." she was frustrated with me now and I knew it by the way she was breathing. "Look fuck a date night. Momma is more important. I understand that this love shit is all new to you and all but were family, remember...? Remember when we were younger and just because your eyes were green and mine were hazel they told us we weren't sisters. Remember momma saying we will always be sisters no matter so fuck that & fuck them. We were to remain tight as Krazy Glue do you remember that Shaye'. Huh, do you...? Well Shaye' I'm fed up with you putting us off for Mr. Wonderful. You need to have your black ass here tomorrow so we can take momma home if not I'm coming to the spot and I'm fucking you up...." and with that she hung up.

I sat in my car and realized I had been doing a lot for Tariq over the course of two months and he's been giving back quite as much but I have been neglecting my family lately. Maybe it was the simple fact and reason I was finally happy and here it was Momma didn't approve and that kind of put a damper on things.

Chapter16

I went ahead and mailed off my applications and went in for my job interview and he loved me. I was hired as the new cashier for lane number 21 in Wal-Mart. I then called Tariq and told him the good news and then I headed over to my hair appointment. Once home I made some cheesy chicken bake and by the time Tariq made it home dinner was ready to be served. I met him at the door as always and kissed him and asked him about his day and of course it was always some drama.

I followed him into the bedroom and helped him to remove his shoes. I then told him his bath water was waiting and that dinner was done. He then stood up and removed his pants and my mouth began to water. "You better go take your bath before-" he approached me and planted his lips on my mind I gave into him...this was our daily routine. He then spun me around and said "Get up on the bed" I crawled up on the bed and on all fours. I felt his strong hands grip my waist my toes curled.

I felt his manhood slowly breech my steaming hydrated starving folds "A-A-A-G-GHHH!!! Ta....Ta....Tarr...TARIQ!" (Smack, Smack) His hips were thrusting up against my backside. My clit swelled as his balls thrashed against it with a riveting vengeance. "TARIQ! TARIQ! TARIQ! OH! OH! SSSSSHHHIIIT! DAMN IT FUUUCK ME OOOOOOOHH!" Tariq bashed away like it was our last day breathing. My breasts swung back n forth helplessly as the pace picked up. Tears rolled down my face as he pushed my back down making *my breast mash into the blanket thus sinking himself that much deeper.*

He grabbed my hair with one hand and a shoulder with the other and pulled fiercely. That was it bulls eye my G-Spot erupted and I felt the wave "OH GOD TARIQ IM....IM...CU...CU....CUMMIN'!! (Splash) "AGGH!" (Splash) "OH PLEASE IT'S...IT'S...TOO" (Splash) "YE-E-EEESSS! THERE OH THERE RIGHT THERE!" (Splash) Ohhhh, Shit..... (Splash) Dammit!!!... (Splash) Tariq right there Papa'....Yes, Yes, Yes....I came for what seemed like an eternity but before I could catch my breath.

I was on my back with my legs up high and my toes pointed towards the ceiling when it happened. I was lost in euphoria I had nowhere to go (Smack, Smack) his hips were moving like jet engine down my runway. "TARIQ PLEASE, PLEASE....OH MY GOD....PLEASE!" My thighs shook, my stomach tightened, and I came yet again my clit screamed in blissful agony I couldn't take much more but Tariq wasn't done. An hour went by and my vision was blurry.

Tariq knelt down and placed two fingers in my center pressing up on my G spot. He then engulfed my concha within his mouth. I thought I was going to pass out as his tongue circled my erect clit building up to yet another explosion. I grabbed his head with both hands as he clamped his lips on my bud. I shook, jolted, quivered "I'M CUMMING....CUMMING....OH TARIQ! But he never let up. The circles of fire turned to vertical lashes of lust. Up and down faster and faster I gasped for air to no avail my eyes clinched shut......Ohhhh, Shit.... (Splash) TAAAAAARRIQQ!!!" Two hours of this left me passed out on the bed.

When I had awaken and managed to crawl to the bathroom. I turned on the shower and adjusted the water temperature and stepped in to some much needed hot water. I sat under that shower nuzzle which seemed to last a lifetime. I heard the doors slid back and I heard "Are you alright Love, You kind of passed out on me" I looked up into his beautiful grey eyes and said "I'm fine, I might have to miss date nite tomorrow because I have to help Tanesha get momma home" he kissed my forehead and said "That's cool, I'll stay here and watch a movie" I held him close to me and prayed this feeling would never end.

I looked up at him "I love you Tariq Gonzalez" and he looked down at me and said "And I love you Ms. Future Gonzalez" we shared a kiss and proceeded with our shower

Chapter 17

The next morning after Tariq left for work I jumped in the Charger and headed to Presbyterian Hospital. When I arrived I was hesitate at first to go up in the elevator but I needed to know what was going on with momma. As I approached I heard her talking to Tanesha "I have no idea what's wrong with that damn girl. She starting to act just like her father, stubborn. I've never known such a stubborn jack ass in all my life. I'm just trying to warn her in advance that there's something wrong with that damn boy but will she listen. Hell Naw, I wish she would wise up and realize that it ain't all what it's cracked up to be"

Tanesha then chimed in "Momma, Tariq seems pretty cool. He's making sure she's filling out her college applications and she just started working down at Wal-Mart. She's doing good momma and you should be proud of her...Momma what's going on really...?" Momma cleared her throat then said "You'll find out soon enough when she gets here matter fact hand me that hat box so I can have it ready for little miss busy body when she gets here" I guess this was my cue to enter the room.

I pushed the door open just as Tanesha was passing momma the hat box. My hands were sweating with anticipation "Hey Momma, Hey Tanesha," I gave each one a hug. "Hey Baby, You have a glow about you" I smiled. She was not finna bait me "So, How is everything going are you ready to go home...?" Momma stretched and said "As soon as the Doctor gets here then we'll see until then have a seat" I sat *down in the available seat next to momma. "Tanesha baby move your chair over here and sit next to your sister" I swallowed because I was nervous as hell now.*

Tanesha moved her chair next to mine and momma spoke as she was removing the top off the infamous hat box "I have been holding on to this for 10yrs now and now I think it's time for you girls to know the truth" and out came a yellow stained envelope. I recognized it right away it was the letter Tanesha had pinned to her jacket that night. "Tanesha baby when you showed up on my door step 10yrs ago I had no idea what to do with you. I was scared and confused so I was unsure. Once I had you off to bed and settled I knew then and only then I had to read this letter. I sat up the whole nite crying and upset but I knew within myself I had to do what was right. I kept my promise and now I share with you this letter" we both reached for the letter. I looked at Tanesha and asked "Are you ready for this...?" she shook her head no but we proceeded. We handled it with caution do to the fact and reason it was so fragile. The letter started as such:

To Whom It May Concern:

I know you don't know me from Adam but I know of you. I met your husband some 10yrs ago in the local lounge located in the city. He was tall handsome and had the most seducing green eyes. I wanted to bed that man something terrible. We had a few drinks and he walked me back to my place. The sex was incredible and if you doubt me I know about the mole on his left ass cheek in the shape of a heart. We had sex on several occasions and that's how I ended up pregnant with Tanesha. Ma'am I'm not writing you this letter as to start up any trouble I just wanted you to know the truth. Marquise told me he would leave you and then marry me but how was I to believe a man that only showed up at my place to have sex with me on occasion. After Tanesha was born he started to come around more often than not with the same empty promises of one day leaving you to no avail. Sooner rather than later he stop coming by to visit he would just randomly call and send me money thru the mail or via Western Union. I later found out once Tanesha had reached the age of three that he moved to New York the bastard.

I did all I could by Tanesha but the jobs were scarce and the welfare was not enough to take care of her needs and hers alone. The waitressing job wasn't paying me enough to make rent let alone bills. I left Tanesha with my mother on occasion to make sure she had a warm place to sleep and enough food to eat but momma got sick *and started to complain. So, I had no choice but to find you and reach out for help. I am so sorry, I tried to do this as long as I could alone but it was too much too soon. I will continue to do for my child what I can if I can I'm so sorry it had to happen this way. If only I was strong enough to make it and pull through. If only I had the strength and the will power but it's hard out here for a recovering addict. Please take care of my daughter and if by chance I would love to see her accomplish something in life. I wish I could of been a better mother but it's so cold and lonely out here when you're going at it alone.*

Ms. Shannon Whelks

Chapter18

I then looked at Tanesha and she was a mess. I grabbed some tissue and passed it to her and I said "It's gonna be alright..." and she just cried. Momma looked at us and said there's more and then she passed us a photo that was contained in the envelope. On the back of the photo it said give to Tanesha.

We looked at this photo and it was a picture of our father. "I'm really gonna kick his ass when I see him. Did you call him yet Shaye'...?" I shook my head no "Well, call him because I have some questions and some answers. I wonder is this why I get this mysterious check every month and if so where is your fucking check...? Why can't he send you any money...? I promise you if it's him then I don't want anything to do with him or his money" I sat there and let her cry and vent as she pleased. Momma looked at us both and said "Tanesha do you think you can handle any more news because if not then I'll wait for a later date" Tanesha blew her nose and wiped her eyes and said "What is it momma...? Could it be more heart wrenching than this..?" Momma hung her head low and said "Baby I'm so sorry I kept all this from you but now is a better time than any to get all this off my chest and then ask for forgiveness before I leave this here old place we call home"

We looked at momma and waited for the other shoe to drop. Momma dug through that hat box and came out with some newspaper clippings she then passed then to Tanesha. The headline read as such: "YOUNG WOMAN FOUND IN AN ABANDON WAREHOSE" we read thru *the article and somewhere towards the end it said witness claim that she left one Shannon Whelks in the dilapidated warehouse after she had a drug overdose. Tanesha threw down the newspaper clippings and ran from the hospital room. I heard momma yelling something about "Let her be Shaye'" but how could I let my sister be after hearing some mess like that.*

I found Tanesha down in the court yard smoking a cigarette and I had never known Tanesha to smoke. "When did you start smoking...?" she looked up at me and said "Right after you decided to leave home and become a house wife. Oh I forgot you're not married your just Tariq's maid" I looked at my sister "Don't start taking shit out on me because your angry. I did nothing to you. I came down here to make sure you were ok but if you wanna start gut checking people I can leave you right here. I don't need this shit from you or from momma. I hate that you just found out your mother was an addict and died of an overdose. That shit is not my fault...You need to take that shit up with momma not me. So when you get thru having your little pity party call me and I'll be on the first thing smoking" I stood up to leave when Tanesha grabbed my hand "Look I'm sorry but look at my life now. The only good thing out of this whole mess is that you are my sister and I love you just the same that will never change. I'm sorry Shaye'" I turned and gave my sister a hug and then my cell rung. "Hello," I heard a bunch of commotion "Hello, Ms. Vines"-"Yes this is Ms. Vines" I heard some more commotion "Ms. Vines is your sister with you...?"-"Yes what's this all about..?" I heard some more noise "Look Ms. Vines your mother just flat lined" I slammed my phone closed and grabbed Tanesha's hand and pulled her along. "Momma just flat lined we have to hurry"

We reached momma's room Dr. Enoch was present "Your mother just had a relapse. We were able to bring her back but she's sleeping now. How about you two go down to the cafeteria and get something to eat. I'll have a nurse call you if she wakes up and wonders where you are" Tanesha and I accepted defeat, tired and weary we turned and headed to the cafeteria.

Chapter19

Tanesha and I sat downstairs in the cafeteria contemplating our next move when my cell rung "Hello," I heard music playing "Hey Love, How's everything going with your mom...?" I explained everything to Tariq and he listened. "Well Love, I'm here if you need me and if you need me to come over and hold your hand I will" I smiled in spite of everything and replied "Naw, I'm good plus I don't want momma to have a brain aneurysm she's going thru enough as if without you showing up. Any-who, I love you I'll be home shortly" he chuckled "Alright, I love you to and I'll be here whenever you need me" and then I closed my cell.

"Why do you always say I'll be home..? Bitch, that's not your place of residence" I looked at my sister "Do you *still have a stick up your ass about early because if you do I can go home right the fuck now" I stood up and started to toward the elevator bank. "Gone sit here and talk to me all greasy, shit, this is not my doing but yet and still I get the fuck you end of the stick. Why is everybody fucking with me all of a sudden? This some bullsh-" the elevator doors opened while I was standing there talking to myself and out stepped Dr. Enoch.*

"Are you leaving Ms. Vines...?" I looked up and said "Yea, I'm outta here. Call me if you need me" he then stopped me and said "Umm, Ms. Vines where would I find your sister...?" I looked at him sideways and first then I said "Oh, Ms. High and Mighty Whelks is over there on her throne having a pity party. I'm outta here, like I said call me if you need me" I

went to step on the elevator and Dr. Enoch stopped me "I forgot to give yo this" he went into his pocket and came out with a folded piece of paper and handed to me. I looked at it and said "What is this...?" he looked at me and said "I don't know exactly but it had your name on it when we went into your mother's room early. I thought you might've wanted it..." and then he turned and walked away. I stuck the paper in my purse and carried my tail upstairs and out to the parking garage.

I pulled into the underground parking garage and then I called Tariq "Hey You, I'm calling because I need you. You did say call when I needed you right...?" he cleared his throat and said "Sure, Where are you and I'll be there in the next 15 minutes" I smiled "I'm in the parking garage"-"I'm on my wa-Did you just say parking garage...?"-"Yea, Why..?"-"Nothing Love, You just had me guessing for a minute. Hell, I was sleep when you called so I was a little disoriented" I shrugged my shoulders "OK I'll be up in a minute"-"OK Cool, I'll be waiting" I rode the elevator up to the 30th floor and I was beat.

When I got off the elevator the first person I saw was Tariq standing there with a bath towel and my pink slippers I could do nothing else but smile. I walked into his embrace and held on for as long as allowed and then and only then did I allow myself to cry. I sat in that tub soaking and I eventually dozed off because the water was now cold and Tariq was knocking on the door and coming in "You OK in here my love" I smiled up at him and said "I'm cool, I just fell asleep is all" he smiled and said "I have something for you to eat once you're done" I looked at him standing there and I couldn't put my finger on it "OK, I'll be out in a second" he backed out and closed the door behind him I proceeded to wash up and got out the tub.

Chapter 20

I threw on one of Tariq's football jersey and went out into the living room and it was all lit up in candles and incense. Tariq came around the corner with a foot basin "What are you doing now...?" he looked at me and said "Sit down right here" I went over to the chair and sat down. "Now place your feet in here" I did as I was asked and then he disappeared. When Tariq returned he had a food tray full of goodies.

He placed the tray across my lap and then he went back into the kitchen. This time he came out with a nice chilled glass of Pepsi and then he kneeled at my feet and said "Your servant waits to please his Queen. Whatever my Queen needs just ask and you lowly servant will provide" I looked at him and smiled. Tariq massaged my feet and I forgot all about eating. Tariq then disappeared into the kitchen and came out with a plate with a covering. I was so wondering what was underneath that top. "Tariq what is this..?" he smiled at me and held up one of his fingers and disappeared again. This time when he came back he had a dozen red and lavender roses and a huge teddy bear.

"Tariq what is all this..." he kissed my lips and said "We've been missing date night for the past couple of weeks. If it's not you taking care of mom's and trying to get your applications together then it's me. Work has been kicking my tail lately and I've been neglecting you and I'm sorry. I had this planned a different way but hey who knows... Mar 'Shaye' Vines I love you and I've never loved anyone as much as I love you now. I would go to the ends of the earth if I could find it and I would leap

because I know within my heart you'll be there to catch me. Shaye' I love you and there is nothing I wouldn't do for you. If you ask me to steal the hope diamond and there's no way I'll make one. Mar 'Shaye' I love you and I know deep inside there is no me without you. You make me complete in every aspect of the word" Tariq reached over and grabbed the plate and turned back and looked at me and presented it to me.

I was nervous has hell right about now plus I looked a hot mess from all the crying "Mar 'Shaye' Vines.....Will You Marry Me....?" and then he removed the top and Oh, My Damn that ring was gorgeous. I looked at Tariq and then the ring. "Yes, Baby....Yes, I'll marry you" I jumped up so fast food went flying everywhere.

Tariq and I made love all thru the night and well into the morning before I was sound asleep. When I woke up it was still early I was extremely thirsty so I went to get me some water when I had the terrible urge to vomit. I ran to the bathroom and make it in the nick of time. I sat there dry heaving for a lifetime it seemed like. Tariq entered the bathroom and held my hair back "Hey Love, What's going on...? Are you alright...?" Tariq let go of my hair and went over to the sink and came back with a cool rag to place at the nape of my neck. He then tied my hair up the best way he could. After crying over into the toilet bowl and dragging myself to the sink to brush my teeth hunger and thirst had passed and all I wanted to do was go back to bed.

Chapter 21

For two days I stayed in bed wondering what was wrong with me. I hadn't heard from Tanesha and momma was still resting so therefore I did the same thing. I called in to my doctor and made an appointment because I had a bad case of the shivers. Tariq called in to work and took a few days off so he could take care of me which was sweet of him. The following day we got up and headed into Oak Park where my doctor told me that not only did I pick up the flu bug but I was also pregnant. I damn near fell off the exam table. Momma was gonna have a conniption when she heard this shit Tanesha as well.

Tariq was overly excited, wow what to do now. Tariq looked at me and said "Are you ready for this my love" I just broke out in tears and that was my answer for everything for the first three months. My dad finally called and told me that he would be in town that following weekend and that he wanted to make sure that it was ok with the family. I didn't wanna say anything but I did manage to tell him momma was in the hospital so it wouldn't be wise to show up just yet. He told me to call him when momma was feeling better so that way we could all sit down and discuss some things. If only he knew that Tanesha was a force to be reckoned with and momma had been off her rocker lately so he had some shit to deal with.

Tanesha finally picked up the phone and called me and said she wanted to come over and talk. I told her sure thing because there was some things we needed to discuss anyway. I told Tariq that

Tanesha was on her way over and he asked if I wanted him to stay but of course I said no, hell I could handle Tanesha. Tariq left for work and I waited on my sister to arrive when I heard the buzzer "Hello,"- "Yes, Ms. Vines...I have your sister here to see you"-"OK Antonio, Send her up"-"Sure thing Ms. Vines" and we disconnected.

I opened the door just a little and wobbled my tail back to the couch. I heard a small knock and I yelled out "Come in!" Tanesha rounded the corner and said "What you not gone stand up and hug your sister" I rocked thru it and stood up big, bold, and beautiful. Tanesha dropped her purse and her keys and started screaming "I'm gonna be an Auntie" over and over. I stood there and smiled while she cried tears of joy. She came over and touched my belly as if she would hurt me. "How far along are you..?" I looked at her and down at my belly "I'm 4 1/2 months now" she bent down to pick up her things and said "Wow, momma and I been tripping that long...?" then she noticed the rock on my finger "Are you in engaged to...?" I shook my head "Did he propose after or before he found out...?" I looked at her and said "Before Nesha" she squealed and said "Imma be Auntie" while doing the cabbage patch.

We sat down and had some lunch and watched movies and by the time Tariq made it home we were back to our regular selves "What's up Brother In-Law" Tanesha stood to give Tariq a hug and he hugged her back. "Babe did you get any dinner fixed...?" I rocked up off the couch and approached him and kissed his lips and said "Well....Umm, No....but I can order us some takeout" he kissed me and said "That's cool, how about Chinese...?" that was fine with me so I dialed the number and ordered enough for seven.

Tanesha stayed well past midnight and Tariq was knocked out. "Look Nesha, you can stay in the guest room if you like. You don't have to leave" but she insisted. I gave Tanesha her hugs and I also asked her "Can u please not tell momma about none of this please. I wanna do it..." Tanesha shook her head "OK" and left.

Chapter 22

I joined Tariq in the bedroom after Tanesha left and he held me as I slept. I woke up that morning to the sound of my cell ringing. "Shaye' momma is up and she wants to see you" I crawled out of bed and replied "Look Nesha, I understand were on the same page and all but momma will never understand" she sighed in frustration "Look Shaye' get your ass down here you have no idea what momma will accept" I threw the covers back on the bed "You told her didn't you....?" Tanesha got really quiet "ANSWER ME NESHA....!!!! You told her didn't you..?" Nesha finally spoke and said "Shaye' I do apologize I was just so damn excited but momma is cool I promise"

I stood up and stretched "Why is it I don't believe you...? Why is it I feel like this is a set up...? I asked you to let me be the one to tell her and you couldn't keep your fucking mouth shut long enough for me to figure the shit out on my own. Fuck You Nesha.....I'm doing this shit when I get good and damn ready...." and I closed my cell and went into the bathroom. I took my shower and got dressed. Today I would find out the sex of my baby and I didn't wanna be late for that appointment.

Once I arrived at the doctor's office Tariq was sitting there waiting "What are you doing here...?" he placed his magazine down and stood up to his feet and said "Umm, today is your prenatal appointment right...? I remember you telling me this morning and I wouldn't miss this for the world. Today is the day I prove you wrong and we find out it's a boy." he smiled this most beautiful smile and I melted. "Hey, sorry for snapping on you, I'm just really moody. Tanesha called today and momma knows and now I have to go by there and do damage patrol. Tanesha said she was OK with the whole thing but I know momma will never be OK when it comes to you. Not saying anything against you but we both know how my momma is...?" I looked up at him as I was signing the sign in sheet.

He rubbed my back and it made me feel a little better if only for a moment. Once my name was called and my cervix was checked and all the necessary poking and prodding, we then went into a small room for the ultrasound. Once the gel was applied then and only then was I able to hear that wonderful sound that sounds like washing machine drums.

The doctor then did some strange maneuvering and said "WOW!!!!" I looked at Tariq and said "What's wrong with our baby Tariq...?" he looked at me and shrugged his shoulders "What the fuck you mean you don't know, find out...?" the nurse then turned to me and said "It's OK Mrs. Gonzalez" that made me smile but I said "It's Ms. Vines could you please tell me what's wrong...?

She then spun the screen around and pointed to the fetus and said "You see this right here this is the fetus heartbeat. Only thing is...." she maneuvered the wand and said "There are two...." I looked up and I heard Tariq say "Holy Shit..." and then he did this whooping hollering thing and then he said "Hey Boo were having twins...." I looked at him and said "I can see that...." the nurse then went on to tell us that they were both boys. Tariq couldn't control his excitement he ran over and kissed the nurse. I looked at him and said "What now....?" he smiled and said "Its okay Boo, I got this..." I was damn sure he did because I was lost for words. How was I gone tell momma I'm pregnant and not only that I was now having twins. Momma was gonna kill me.....

Chapter 23

Tariq walked me to my car and kissed my forehead "It's gonna be okay Boo, I promise..." I then crawled in my car and rubbed my belly. I was damn near on the verge of tears when my cell phone rung. I looked at the caller id and it was daddy calling "Hi Daddy," he was hesitant but he said "Hi Sweetie How is everything...?" I then told him momma was woke and I told him there was some things we needed to discuss and there were some questions that needed answering.

I then told him that I wanted him to meet someone because my future depended on me being happy. He then said "Well, I have some good news I'll be back in town on the 21st that's next weekend and hopefully this finds your mother in good health. I want to sit down with the both of you and discuss some things as far as why I left and why I have returned. I'm not sick or anything so don't worry your pretty little head about that. So, I'll call you sometime next week to make sure everything is cool before I show up at your doorstep" I breathed a sigh of relief and said "Sure thing daddy, I'll be in touch" I then hung up the phone and started towards momma's.

I pulled the Monte' Carlo into the drive way and out came Tanesha. "Look we need to discuss something Missy, I understand you're pregnant and moody but you just can't be-" her words froze in her throat when she noticed the tears in my eyes. "Daddy just called me and said he'll be in town next weekend. Tariq just kissed me and went back to work and the nurse said that I was having not one baby but two. Tanesha please tell me what the fuck imma do with two babies. Imma baby my damn self. What the fuck Tanesha...?" all I could do was cry.

"I celebrated my birthday with Tariq and it was lovely but it would have been better if you and momma were present. Tariq did everything imaginable to make me happy, diamonds, new whip, had my hair and nails done. He hired a masseuse, then on top off all that he had a chef come out to the house and make my favorite meal and I couldn't enjoy it. Now here I am engaged and about to have a family of my own and all I want is you and momma there thru it all..." Tanesha held me and let me cry "It's okay Shaye'" I snatched away from her and said "I'm tired of it's gonna be okay. I'm tired of hearing those words. All I hear is its okay. Fuck It's Okay" I

then turned and jumped in my car and drove over to the rocks and had a good cry.

Chapter 24

I arrived home late that night and Tariq was up waiting and worried "Babe, What's the matter...?" I looked at Tariq and shook my head and said "You know what you'll never understand.." he gave me the screw face and said "Try Me" I sat there and explained to him that I missed my family and that I left home with the intentions of one day going back. I told him it had been damn near a year and that I was at my wits end about everything.

I wanted my momma back and I wanted the relationship me and my sister once shared and now I didn't have those things. I told him how much I loved him and I only wanted what we had to work if only my mother could accept it. I told him how scared I was at 19 with not one but two babies on the way and how I got tired of everybody telling me it was gonna be okay. I cried and I yelled and I screamed until I was damn near horse and then I passed out right there in the middle of the living room floor.

I woke up with Tariq sitting beside me in the rocker I bought a week ago. "Babe, I'm so sorry you're going thru all this. I never meant for any of this to happen. I love you too much not to at least try to make this right. First thing tomorrow morning I'll call into work and then we can go to your mothers together and try to explain the fact that we are engaged and the fact simple fact and reason that you are pregnant with twins. I think your mother will accept the fact that were engaged and she'll get past it she just has to. Do anyone realize that this is taking a toll on you and I don't like it one bit" I looked at Tariq and realized the tears in his eyes and I reached out my hands to him and he joined me on the bed. "We don't have to go to mommas in the morning. She's still in the hospital she should be home shortly; let me be the first to tell her everything. Then and only then you can make your presence known and place all your cards at her mercy. I believe that if she hears you out she'll understand you better" I rolled over on my side and kissed his lips and snuggled into his arms and fell back to sleep.

Chapter 25

The weekend was slowly approaching and momma was finally home and we talked over the phone constantly but I never went to visit. She asked me over and over again when I was coming and I always said soon. My pregnant belly was way outta control and if I didn't tell momma soon Lord help me. My dad called and wanted to let me know that he would be in town for sure that weekend. I told him it was cool and I was looking forward to seeing him but yet and still I had to call momma.

Whew, this was gonna be a hard one: I picked up my phone and called momma "Hello," Tanesha answered "Hey Tanesha, Can you put momma on...?" she smacked her lips "What's this...? You got an attitude with me now...? No Hi Tanesha, No

Nothing...? Just can you put momma on...?" I developed a new habit over the course of months and that was smacking my lips as well "Look Nesha, I don't have time for this shit put momma on the phone..." Tanesha then threw the phone down on the table and I could hear her hollering for momma to pick up the phone "Hey Baby," I took a deep breath and started in "Momma, Daddy just called and said that he would be here this weekend and he wanted to know if we could meet at your place and if so I need to call him back and let him know" momma took and deep breath and started counting that wasn't a good sign.

"Look Shaye' if your dad wants to meet you here then that's fine with me. Did you tell him about Tanesha...?" I looked at the phone in shock and said "No Ma'am"-

"That's good. I'm only saying that because he needs to see this for himself. He needs to know that I took care of his responsibilities while his ass was out trolloping around with some whore" I cleared my throat and said "Momma wait. What whore..?" she then changed the subject and said "I'll see you this weekend baby. Bye" and she hung up. "Ain't this some shit...?"

I prepared myself for the infamous smack down when I arrived at mommas earlier and I was nervous standing on that porch trying to cover up my belly. The door swung open and there stood momma with a look on her face that was between confusion and blind fury "Shaye' Oh My Baby" she stretched out her arms to embrace me and I cried tears of joy for the simple fact and reason I needed this but I also a little confused because I was waiting for the slap across the face.

I went into the house like a stranger and Tanesha came around the corner with her boy shorts on and her cigarette dangling from her lips "Mar 'Shaye'" I looked at her and said "Tanesha" and she went into the kitchen. Momma looked at me and said "Do you want something to drink baby...?" I looked at my momma kinda strange and said "Sure" Momma went into the kitchen and I could hear her yelling at Tanesha about being rude to me and that no matter what we were still sisters even if I was stubborn and unruly.

Momma came outta the kitchen and said "Sorry baby Tanesha is bringing you something to drink. So, let me see this ring...?" I showed her my ring cautiously and she smiled and "Oh Baby I'm so proud of you" I looked at momma and thought: What the fuck is going on here..? Tanesha came out carrying a tray full of different juices, sodas, and ice tea "For you Your Highness, Take your pick" this bitch was on my last nerve "Look Nesha I don't know what the fuck your problem is but whatever it is, it needs to cease to exist because I've done nothing to you. Every sense you found out about your dad and your momma you've been nothing but a bitch towards me. Get over yourself and act like your 21 instead of 12" I picked up the ice tea off the tray and momma begin her reign of terror.

Chapter 26

"I want both of y'all to sit y'all asses down and listen to me" Tanesha went to open her mouth and momma said "Shut up and sit your ass down" I knew it was coming because she was being too nice. "Now, I'm tired of running around here being nice and not saying what's been on my mind these past few weeks I've been home. I'm tired of you young lady..." she said pointing at Tanesha "Running around here acting like somebody owe you something. I don't owe you shit but an apology for withholding information.

I'm damn tired of you two witches walking around here at each other's throat and Tanesha when did you start smoking them stankin ass cigarettes" Tanesha went to speak "Shut up dammit, I told y'all when y'all were younger that just because one is lighter than the other and your eyes are hazel and hers is green doesn't mean shit. You were to remain sisters thru and thru and you two stupid wenches done forgot what I done drilled into y'all's head" she then looked at me "And you my beautiful naive daughter, I love you no more and no less than I do your sister but your just plum stupid to think reasonably.

I've tried to warn you about Tariq and your ass just wouldn't listen. I tried to tell your ass he wasn't right and your stubborn ass just kept on thinking that I was old and stupid. Well guess what sweetheart I have yo' ticket punched" she then looked at Tanesha and said "Go get my damn hatbox" Tanesha got up and went into momma's bedroom just when the doorbell rang.

I looked at momma and said "I'll get it" she sat there and rocked back and forth and said "Gone right ahead, Gone right ahead" I went to the door and opened and there stood the man I called daddy "Daddy" he looked at me in all my splendor and said "Mar 'Shaye'" and he stretched out his hand and touched my belly and the babies kicked.

"Daddy, Please come in everyone is in the living room we have so much to discuss" Daddy followed me into the living room and there momma stood and he said "Gladys" and momma looked at him said "You a bastard you know that..." he looked at her and said "I deserved that" she then looked at him and said "How could you...After 10yrs...How dare you show your face and then come up in my house like everything is okay...? You have some

nerve you know that some nerve..." just then Tanesha rounded the corner and said "Here you go momma" I was sitting on the couch when daddy said "Momma" and momma said "Yea, Momma....Meet your daughter" and she stepped to the side to reveal Tanesha.

Tanesha dropped the hatbox and looked at him and lunged at him. Momma grabbed her and said "Tanesha now is not the time for this shit. Now is the time to get down to the bottom of the barrel" Tanesha looked at daddy and said "You knew about me all along. You knew I was here for the simple fact and reason you kept sending me those checks. Why, Huh, Why.....? Answer Me...!!!!" momma was doing one hell of a job holding Tanesha back "Look were all upset here and I understand there is a lot of questions needing to be answered. Maybe we should just sit down and discuss this like adults" everyone looked at me and Tanesha said "Shut up Shaye'" so I just sat back and finished drinking my tea.

Chapter 27

Momma looked at me and then Tanesha and said "Look I know were all upset but let's let your father have a say" Daddy looked around at the women present and he first acknowledge momma "Gladys, I'm so sorry I left when I did there was so much going on that you didn't know about..." momma said under her breath "I know that's right" daddy then continued "I had developed a habit a terrible habit. I started drinking and hanging with my co-workers down at the plant and on some nights I dappled in a little "X" I was high outta my mind on most occasions. I developed a habit for the fast life and the fast women. I wanted the seduction and the pleasure of both worlds.

That's when I met Shannon and we hit it off lovely she was attentive and she made sure my every sexual fantasy was fulfilled. When she told me she was pregnant I didn't know how to react so I panicked and I lied and told her that me and you were getting a divorce and then me and her could be together. You were always working and you never had time for me and when you did it was limited because you spent all your time with Shaye'.

I felt neglected and put out by my own I was like a child fighting for attention. Since I couldn't get that attention from you I got it from Shannon even if I did have to lie about the circumstance between us" he took a pause in his speech and Tanesha sat there tapping her foot and smoking her cigarette "You know what you bastard I don't know what my momma ever saw in you. Yea, she said she adored your eyes and your sex appeal but you know what you're a taker not a giver. You took from my momma and in the midst of you taking from her she lost me because she had nothing to give. She turned to a life of drugs and alcohol because of you and your lies. Oh My God, I just figured it out it was your doing wasn't it, it was you who turned my mother on to the drugs" Tanesha stood and daddy put his head down and that made him more obvious "You bastard it was you I can't believe this shit. My momma died in an abandon building of an overdose and it was all you're doing for turning her on to this lifestyle. UGH, I HATE YOU!!!!!......" and she lunged at him and me and momma dived for her before she made it over the table.

Chapter 28

My father sat there and said real soft like "I'm so sorry Tanesha..." Tanesha looked at him fuming with tears streaming down her face and said "Sorry, Sorry, this motherfucka says he's sorry. Well, you know what you fuckin bastard I don't want your fuckin sorry. I don't want shit from you..." she then stood up and went for the stairs. Momma yelled after her "Tanesha get yo' black ass back here" and she kept walking. Daddy then looked at me and said "Mar 'Shaye', I'm sorry that all this came about. I'm sorry, I never explained to you what really happened between me and your mother.

I'm sorry I wasn't there for any of your accomplishments. I wanna be here though for the birth of my grandchild if you'll have me" I looked towards momma and then I looked towards my daddy and said "Daddy, there's so much I wanna say to you right now but do to the simple fact and reason so much has transpired. I have one question: Why...? Why was I the last one to find out about everything....? You sent Tanesha money every month what was that guilt trip money. Momma sat here and cried her eyes out just about every other night after you left. Then no more than a few months later Tanesha shows up with that damn note and she started crying again.

I had no idea what she was going thru until recently when we read that same letter. Momma worked two jobs at least constantly to make sure me and Tanesha were taken care of. We never knew us being sisters were actually true until recently but momma raised us to believe we were nothing more than just that, sisters. You know what daddy I'm pregnant with twins and they will know one grandparent and that's momma. She has earned it..." Daddy put his head down and said "There's more" momma threw her hands up in surrender and at that time my cell rung.

"Hello," it was Tariq "Hey Love, How is everything going so far...?" I looked at momma and then daddy and then said "You know what you can come get me because I done said all I have to say and in doing so you can meet my dead beat daddy" Tariq cleared his throat and said "I should be there in the next 25 minutes" I told him I loved him and then I hung up. Momma then turned to me and said "Is Tariq on his way...?" I looked at her strangely and said "Yea momma he's on

his way...." she looked at me and said "Good" she then turned to my father and said "So, Marquise tell me about the third woman in your life" he looked at momma and said "How did you know about her...?" Momma smiled and pulled yet another envelope out of the hatbox "I found out when I received this letter but by the time I got this one your little surprise was already snatched up and in your custody"

My father read the note to himself and said "Have you...?" she shook her head no "So tell me or I'll tell your little secret because I know for damn sure this one is gonna hurt you more than it's gonna hurt me and in the process destroy lives. So get to talking you slimy bastard" my father looked at me and said "Shaye' could you please excuse me and your mother please....? Just for a second" I looked at momma and she gave me the head nod so I wobbled my tail into the kitchen to wait for Tariq.

Chapter 29

I heard momma and daddy yelling about why didn't you tell me and you need to tell the girls because this is bullshit and then the doorbell rang. "Shaye' come get this damn door" I wobbled out of the kitchen and out thru the hallway and to the door. I looked up and Tanesha was at the foot of the stairs when I opened the door and Tariq walked in. Tanesha looked at me and gave me a hug and said "I love you Shaye' and I'm so sorry. Can you ever forgive me for being an ass...?" I hugged her back and said "Sure Nesha, I love you more than life itself I wouldn't know what to do without you and momma" she then broke our in embrace and rubbed my belly and the babies kicked.

She giggled and said "Oh wow, they kicked for me" she then looked at Tariq and said "What's up brother in law...?" he smiled and said "Hey Sis" and they gave each other a hug. I heard momma yelling for me "Girl get your black ass in her so your daddy can see this man you gone marry..." I looked at Tariq and said "You ready...?" he looked at me and said "Yea, let's go" he kissed my forehead and grabbed my hand and Tanesha grabbed the other one.

When we walked into the room daddy was there sitting in the chair with his back to me and momma was sitting there like she had just won the lottery. "Daddy I would like for you to meet my fiancé" as daddy stood to his feet and spun around to greet Tariq the world came to a standstill "It's nice to meet you...." Daddy's jaw drop and he said "Tariq...?" Tariq then looked at him and said "Daddy...?" I looked at

167

Tariq and said "What the shit you mean daddy....?" Tanesha looked at daddy and Tariq standing side by side and said "This is some scary shit" she then looked at momma and said "You knew didn't you...? All this time you knew and didn't say anything. You know what your one cruel ass woman to sit here and let this shit happen"

I then looked at daddy with tears in my eyes "Explain Daddy.....? Explain this shit.....? EXPLAIN DAMMIT.....?" my daddy looked at me and said "Mar 'Shaye' this is what I came here to tell you. I called Tariq earlier and told him I was in town and that we needed to talk. I was trying to correct my wrongs and I ended up being too late...." I looked at momma and said "How could you, you knew all along that's why you resented him so much, that's why *you were always pushing him away. Why not tell me that momma...? Why not tell me that the man that I'm in love with and finna marry is my brother. Huh Momma....? I'm pregnant and now I find out this shit, don't you think it's a little too late now momma"* *she looked at me and said "Shaye' I've been trying to get you to sit down and go thru this box for a year now and every time there's a distraction. I wanted you to find out for yourself. I didn't want you to find out this way. I promise you I didn't"*

I looked at my momma and said "You didn't want me to find out this way, that didn't stop you from smiling like a Cheshire cat when we walked in here. You know what momma; fuck you and daddy you can burn in hell for all I give a damn." I looked at Tariq and I pulled the ring from my finger and gave it back to him. I then looked down at my protruding stomach and wished like hell that this was all one huge nightmare. "Tariq I'm truly sorry. You were everything to me. You were attentive, loving, kind, sweet and a gentleman. I'm so sorry all this had to happen. I guess were all some sorry mutha-fucka's huh...?" I then turned to Tanesha and said "I love you so much I guess now two makes three. Who would have ever thought I would lose my virginity to my brother, fall in love and get pregnant..? I guess we have our parents to thank for fucking shit up for us huh....?" I then looked at my family and headed upstairs.

I went into my room and locked the door. I then stretched out on the bed. I felt my stomach churning and I knew I had to puke so I ran for the bathroom. After my stomach was empty and I was left with nothing but dry heaves I thought of my babies. I pulled off all my clothes and then plugged the tub up and ran me some much needed bath water. I then grabbed me some aspirin out of the medicine cabinet and popped two and crawled into the tub to relax.

Chapter 30

I was feeling light headed and I did remember feeling a bit woozy. Whew, how many of these things did I take..? I only remembered taking two. I heard my name being called but it felt like it was coming from a tunnel. I walked towards the voice and the closer I got the further it seemed. "Shaye' please baby wake up don't do this. Come back to me Shaye' please...?" I heard Tariq's voice but I had no idea how to find him. "SOMEONE CALL THE FUCKIN AMBULANCE!!!!!!" Tariq was yelling "I'm on the phone with them now" said Tanesha. "Shaye' please stay with me think about the babies. Come on babe stay with me" I could hear Tariq crying but I wanted to go near the water and sit down and put my feet in and feel the sun on my face. "What has she consumed Tariq...?"

Tanesha was asking. Tariq picked up the bottle "Tylenol P.M. and I have no idea how many" Tanesha delivered the message.

I could hear them fussing over me but who cared this was the life. The sirens grew louder as they approached the house. Tanesha rushed downstairs and snatched the door open. "She's upstairs" Tanesha led the way. I was sitting on the bank with my feet in the water when I felt my body being lifted and placed on something cold. I heard Tariq say "Be careful with her DAMMIT!!!!!!" I was being wheeled out of the house and I could hear Tanesha say "I'm riding with y'all".

When I came to Tanesha was sitting there looking glum. "How long have I been here and where is momma" Tanesha jerked her head my way and said "Girl, you had me worried. You've been here sleeping for three weeks now. The babies are fine of course. The nurses have been monitoring you off and on. I've been here by your side praying that you would wake up because I wouldn't know what to do if you ever left me. Any-who, Momma she felt bad by not telling you the truth and said if you never returned home she'll understand and daddy humph, he left town a little after Tariq broke his nose. Girl that was the funniest shit I've ever saw but that's a whole nother' story in itself.

What were you thinking about, taking all them damn pills anyway...? Anyway, Tariq knew something was wrong so after he called your name countless times with no answer. He finally kicked down the door only to find you on the verge of no return. Girl, you scared me to death. Oh and speaking of Tariq he asked me to give you this" she pulled an enveloped from her pocket and passed it to me. It had his name written across the front and I automatically put it up to my nose and inhaled his scent and then I opened it....

Chapter 31

Dear Love,

I hope this letter finds you in good health. Everything I ever told you was the truth. I never loved anyone the way I loved you. It's a shame that now that we found love none of it even matters any more. I gonna miss you but I had to pack up and leave and no I won't tell you where I lay my head because it's hard enough laying it hear without you. I pray that you find it in your heart to find love again and do me a favor and take care of the babies. Hell, I don't know what my title even is....on one hand I'm a father and on the other I'm a uncle. This shit is all screwed up and no I don't want you to give them up for adoption. No, don't give them to your sister....We'll figure this out one way or another. Our father screwed us all...Now I have two kids and two new sisters....Ha!

Well, I know you don't wanna talk about it let alone think about it but I'll always be here in the shadows whenever you need me and do me a favor tell Tanesha to stop biting her nails it ain't cute.....(Smile)

Tariq

I looked over at Tanesha and there she was nibbling away at her nails. Tariq says stop that it's not lady like. We both looked at each other and shared a laugh. "I'm gonna miss him Nesha"-"I know baby but we'll get through this together I promise" she crawled up in the hospital bed behind me and we fell asleep......

Thank you for taking this ride with me. In the mist of everything good, I'll always have GOD, my babies, and my pen...#BlackRose

Coming Soon:

Deception: The Other Side

Lesbian: Come Walk With Me

Sextasies:

Short Stories & Poems

www.ingramcontent.com/pod-product-compliance
Lightning Source LLC
Chambersburg PA
CBHW072124170626

46813CB00004B/1688